WARNING!

Scaredy Squirrel insists that everyone brush their teeth with germ-fighting toothpaste before reading this book.

...tist, Rosa, and for Manuel
...Valerie, my friend and publisher,
...seven inspiring years

Published by

Happy Cat Books

An imprint of Catnip Publishing Ltd

Islington Business Centre

3-5 Islington High Street

London N1 9LQ

This edition first published in 2007

1 3 5 7 9 10 8 6 4 2

First published in Canada by Kids Can Press Ltd, 29 Birch Avenue,
Toronto, ON M4V 1E2

Text and illustrations copyright © Melanie Watt, 2007

The moral rights of the author/illustrator have been asserted

A CIP catalogue record for this book is available from the British library

ISBN 978-1-905117-57-4

The artwork in this book was rendered in charcoal pencil and acrylic
The text is set in Potato Cut

Printed in China

Scaredy Squirrel

makes a friend

Melanie Watt

HAPPY CAT BOOKS

Scaredy Squirrel doesn't have a friend.
He'd rather be alone than risk encountering
someone dangerous. A squirrel could get bitten.

A few individuals Scaredy Squirrel is afraid to be bitten by:

walruses

bunnies

beavers

piranhas

Godzilla

So Scaredy Squirrel
finds interesting ways
to pass the time all
by himself.

He reads.

He whistles.

He crafts.

He yawns.

He knits.

He chats.

He counts.

Until one day he spots ...

The Perfect Friend
(according to Scaredy Squirrel)

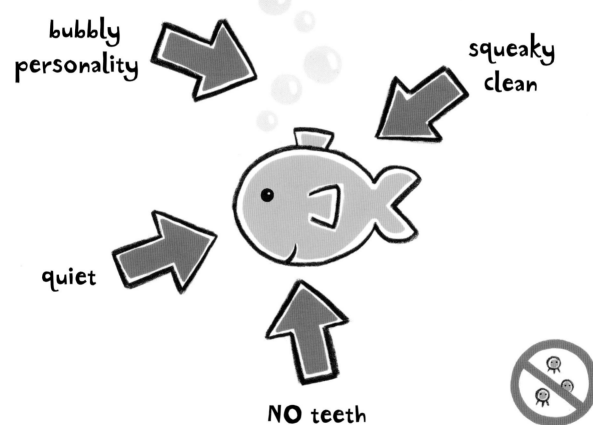

bubbly personality

squeaky clean

quiet

NO teeth

germ-free

Doesn't do much, **BUT** is 100% safe!

A few items Scaredy Squirrel needs to make the Perfect Friend:

lemon	name tag	mittens	comb

mirror	air freshener	toothbrush	chew toy

How to make the Perfect First Impression:

tame bad hair

brush teeth thoroughly
and practice smile
(check for nutty breath
and food caught
between teeth)

prepare
freshly
squeezed
lemonade

wear mittens
to hide
sweaty paws

HELLO
my name is
Scaredy

make sure
name tag
is visible

use pine scent
to smell
delightful

follow the Perfect Plan ⇨

The Perfect Plan

Step 1: Toss down chew toy to distract biters

Step 2: Use mirror to check hair and teeth

Step 3: Run to fountain

Step 4: Point to name tag and smile

Step 5: Offer lemonade

Step 6: Make the Perfect Friend

I am here.

Key

✖	nut tree
	fountain
	tree
	rocks
	bush
	pine tree
	pond
	biter
	biter
	biter
	biter
	biter

Don't talk to suspicious bunnies.

Stay away from piranha-infested ponds.

Beware of walruses: they're fast on their flippers.

Goldfish is here.

Avoid beavers: they could snap at any moment.

Watch out for Godzilla — for obvious reasons!

BUT let's say, just for example, that Scaredy Squirrel **DID** come face to face with a potential biter. He knows exactly what **NOT** to do ...

 **DO NOT** show fear.

 **DO NOT** show your fingers.

 **DO NOT** make eye contact.

 **DO NOT** make any loud noises.

 If all else fails, **PLAY DEAD** ...

And hand over the Test.

objects in mirror are closer than they appear

And he realizes . . .

The dog chases Scaredy around the bush . . .

around the fountain . . .

Time out!

and around in circles . . .

until Scaredy Squirrel . . .

Plays DEAD.

30 minutes later

1 hour later

2 hours later

After all this time,
Scaredy Squirrel
realizes that the
dog doesn't want
to bite him ...

He just wants a friend!

Scaredy Squirrel points to his name tag and smiles.

Then he starts chasing his new buddy.

They play fetch.

They play hide-and-seek.

And they play dead.

Scaredy Squirrel forgets all about the goldfish, not to mention the walruses, bunnies, beavers, piranhas and Godzilla.

Time flies when you're having fun!

All this excitement
inspires Scaredy
Squirrel to make a few
minor changes to his
idea of a friend ...

My Almost Perfect Friend
(according to Scaredy Squirrel)

wet doggy smell

muddy paws

tooth

loud bark

drool

germs

83% safe, but LOTS OF FUN!

P.S. As for the
wet doggy smell,
it's been taken care of.